DATE DUE

BRODART, CO. Cat. No. 23-221

DISNEY PRESS
LOS ANGELES • NEW YORK

INTRODUCTION

Somewhere out there, in a bedroom much like yours, there was a girl who loved to build things with her LEGO bricks.

She had already built all the princess castles, so she decided to combine them and make a brand-new, super-special castle. Each day, she designed the castle a little differently, always changing it and imagining new ways for it to be magical.

In fact, it was the most magical, wonderful castle she had ever seen, but it was missing something—the princesses. Since this girl also loved the Disney Princesses, she put many of them into the castle, too.

Now the only thing left to do was make up story after story about her favorite princesses—and some new friends—having amazing adventures at the ever-changing castle.

This is one of those stories. . . .

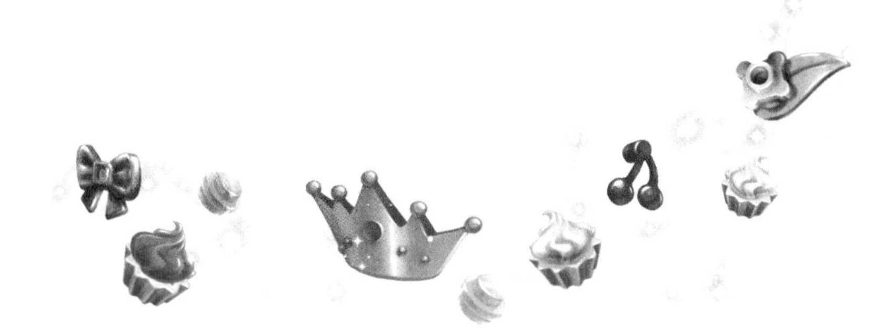

CHAPTER 1

One morning, Cinderella, Mulan, Ariel, and Snow White were playing hide-and-seek. It was their favorite game to play inside the magical castle because there were so many places to hide.

When it was Cinderella's turn to seek, she stood at the top of the staircase, closed her eyes, and counted to ten.

Then she called out, "Ready or not, here I come!"

Now, it's important to remember that the princesses who lived in this castle were all best friends. So Cinderella knew exactly where to look for everyone. She knew that Mulan liked to hide in the warrior training room.

Ariel liked to hide behind a bed.

And Snow White liked to hide in the castle gardens, where she could be close to her animal friends.

Cinderella decided to look for Mulan first.

But as she was coming down the stairs, something unusual caught her eye. She let out a huge gasp.

At the bottom of the stairs, there was a brand-new door that Cinderella had never seen before.

Cinderella smiled to herself and thought, *What could possibly be behind that door?*

CHAPTER 2

The best thing about living in a magic, ever-changing castle was that . . . well, it was magic. And ever-changing. There were always new things to discover. New rooms and new passageways. Sometimes the princesses would wake up to find their rooms in a whole new place!

Which was why, after Cinderella had gathered all the other princesses and they stood in front of the mysterious new door, everyone was very excited.

“Does anyone want to guess what’s behind the door before I open it?” Jasmine asked. She was always the first one to take charge.

"Maybe a new reading room!" said Belle.

"Or an art studio!" said Rapunzel.

"Or an indoor lagoon, with giant waterslides and a dolphin fountain!" said Ariel.

"Maybe . . ." said Mulan doubtfully. "Let's open it and find out!"

Slowly, Jasmine reached out and turned the door handle. The girls all peered through the doorway, their eyes wide and curious.

"Oh, my!" said Aurora. "It's a ballroom!"

"Woo-hoo!" cried Cinderella.

They all agreed that a ballroom was pretty amazing.

"I know exactly what we should do with it," said Cinderella. Her friends turned to her.

"Let me guess. Throw a ball?" said Jasmine.

Cinderella smiled. "No. We should have a slumber party! Because when you have a slumber party, you get to stay up late." She grinned. "*Past* midnight."

"That does sound exciting," Ariel agreed.

"It's official," said Cinderella. "The Magical Castle Slumber Party shall be tonight!"

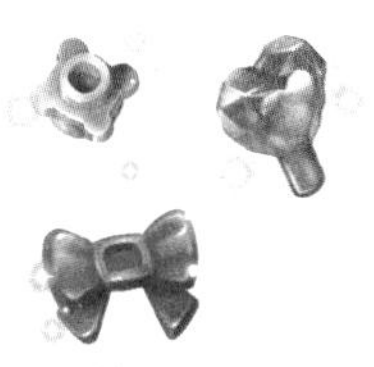

CHAPTER 3

Not far from the castle, in a small lair in the forest, there happened to live a very nice dragon. Well, she was nice when she wasn't hungry. But who *is* really nice when they're hungry?

The dragon had lived in the forest near the castle for as long as anyone could remember.

While the princesses were busy planning their slumber party, the dragon was busy planning her day. She had a *lot* planned. She was going to eat some sweets—she loved sweets.

She was going to fly around the forest.

And she was going to breathe some fire.

You know, normal dragon things.

But when the dragon flew over the castle, she noticed something unusual. The castle had a new room! A giant room with beautiful stained glass windows.

I wonder what that could be? thought the dragon. *I'd better go investigate.*

And just like that, the dragon forgot all about her big plans.

CHAPTER 4

Inside the castle, the preparations for the slumber party had begun.

Cinderella was hard at work building a chandelier to hang from the high ceiling. Mulan was decorating the ballroom with string lights and purple flowers. Rapunzel was painting a majestic mural on the wall.

Belle was looking through books to find spooky stories to read. And Ariel was bringing in comfy blankets and pillows.

It was definitely going to be an epic slumber party.

But as Ariel walked by the windows, she noticed something outside the castle, on the garden wall.

"Is that a . . . ?" Ariel's eyes widened. "It is! Everyone, come look! There's a dragon out there!"

The princesses ran to the window to look.

"We should invite the dragon to the slumber party!" Ariel said.

"Yes!" agreed Snow White. "She looks really lonely."

"I like this idea," said Cinderella. "I know exactly how it feels to be left out."

"No," said a voice from the corner. The princesses all looked over to see Aurora shaking her head. "Dragons cannot be trusted!"

"Come on," urged Belle. "You shouldn't be so quick to judge her from the outside. Some scary-looking creatures can turn out to be nice."

"Hmm," said Mulan thoughtfully. "I might have to agree with Aurora. Dragons *can* be a bit unpredictable."

The princesses all looked at each other. Jasmine took charge. "Let's vote. All in favor of inviting the dragon?"

Everyone raised her hand. Well, everyone except Aurora.

Even Mulan eventually put her hand in the air.

"It's settled," said Jasmine. "The dragon is coming to the party! Maybe she'll have so much fun, she'll want to stay forever and be our castle pet!"

She flashed a kind smile at Aurora. "Don't worry. Everything will be okay—you'll see."

But Aurora did not look convinced. Not at all.

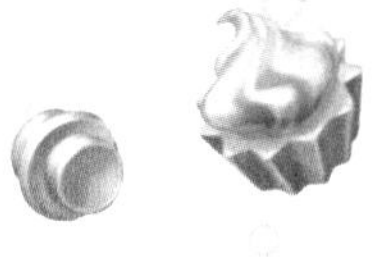

At that very moment, just outside the front door, someone was walking up the steps.

It was the Mysterious Messenger.

The princesses all *loved* the Mysterious Messenger. She always brought very interesting messages. Interesting—and mysterious.

That day the message was especially important, which was why the Mysterious Messenger knocked urgently on the castle door.

Thump! Thump! Thump!

Then she waited.

When there was no answer, the Mysterious Messenger knocked again—this time even louder.

THUMP! THUMP! THUMP!

But the door remained closed. And that was because, inside the castle, the princesses were so busy talking about inviting the dragon to the slumber party that no one heard the thumping at the door.

Beware!
The dragon
is not a pet!

This was a *very* important message. It *had* to be given to the princesses. So the Mysterious Messenger knocked a third time, the loudest of them all.

THUMP! THUMP! THUMP!

Finally, when there was still no answer, she decided to write the message on a piece of paper and slip it under the door.

Unfortunately, the note slid right under the fancy rug, where no one could see it.

It had been settled. The dragon would be invited to the party and hopefully want to stay as the new castle pet.

"But how will we get the dragon into the castle?" asked Ariel.

"I have an idea!" Mulan said, raising her hand in the air as she always did when she had an idea.

"Dragons love sweets! Let's invite her to the party with a cupcake."

"Perfect!" cried Cinderella.

So all the princesses (except Aurora, of course) set off into the forest with a cupcake in search of the dragon's lair.

If the princesses had seen the note left by the Mysterious Messenger, they would have stopped their plans immediately. They would never have left the castle to find the dragon's lair.

And they would never, *ever* have invited the dragon to the slumber party with a cupcake.

But the princesses did *not* see the note.

In fact, they all stepped right *over* it on their way out the front door.

CHAPTER 8

The dragon's lair was a small cave surrounded by trees. However, the dragon had not yet returned home for the day. Cinderella frowned. "It looks a little plain."

Ariel shrugged. "Maybe dragons like plain things."

Snow White placed the cupcake and the invitation in front of the cave, and the princesses all quickly returned to the castle to start the slumber party.

And to wait.

They didn't have to wait very long. They had barely spread their sleeping bags on the floor when there was a knock on the big ballroom doors.

THUMP! THUMP! THUMP!

This time, the princesses heard the knock.

"Hooray!" yelled Jasmine. "The dragon has arrived!"

"I still think this is a bad idea," said Aurora.

Snow White looked at the dragon waiting outside. "She looks friendly."

"Let's let her in!" said Cinderella.

She ran to the doors to open them.

"Welcome to our slumber party!" said Cinderella, holding the doors open wide.

There's something you should probably know about dragons. They take up a *lot* of space. Once the dragon entered the ballroom, there was hardly any room left for the princesses!

"I don't like this," said Aurora to Mulan.

While the rest of the princesses were admiring the dragon's large feet and long tail, Aurora and Mulan were standing as far away from the dragon as possible.

"What if the dragon sneezes? And *fire* shoots out?!" Aurora asked.

"I have an idea," Mulan said for the second time that day.

"What is it?" asked Aurora.

Mulan pointed to the hallway that led to the kitchen. "Follow me."

CHAPTER 10

The six other princesses didn't notice that Mulan and Aurora had left the ballroom. They were too busy introducing themselves to the dragon. The dragon looked happy.

Then Cinderella had an announcement to make. "Time to make s'mores!" she said.

Jasmine and Rapunzel brought over the marshmallows, graham crackers, and chocolate. Snow White showed the dragon and Ariel how to place the marshmallow on the roasting stick. Neither one of them had ever made s'mores before.

Everyone had her stick ready.
But there was one big problem.
"There's no fire," said Belle.

"Dragon!" Ariel said. "Will *you* light the fireplace?"

The dragon smiled, happy to help. The princesses all scooted back as the dragon leaned forward. She sucked in a big breath and blew!

Fire shot out of her mouth! But it was too much—it burnt the marshmallows to a crisp. And it singed the edges of the blankets nearby!

"Uh-oh," said Ariel. "Maybe s'mores weren't such a good idea after all."

CHAPTER 11

Later, the dragon was happily roasting her s'mores in the fireplace. She didn't seem bothered by the marshmallow mishap. And why would she have been? Dragons aren't afraid of fire.

The princesses, however, had gathered in the corner to talk.

“Do you think this was a good idea?” asked Snow White, looking worried.

“Maybe dragons aren’t supposed to be inside,” said Rapunzel.

“Don’t be silly!” said Cinderella with a big smile. “It was just some burnt marshmallows. Everything is going to be great! This is still going to be the best slumber party ever!”

"Hmm," said Jasmine. She leaned back against the table, and one of the plates slid off and made a loud *CRASH!*

It echoed all over the ballroom.

Now, dragons might not be afraid of fire, but they certainly do get startled easily. The dragon roared in surprise and leapt into the air. She flew all over the ballroom, knocking into everything!

Tables were knocked over, decorations were ripped down, and even the beautiful chandelier Cinderella had built came crashing to the ground.

The princesses screamed.

"This party suddenly became very *un*fun," said Ariel.

* * *

Meanwhile, in the castle kitchen, Aurora and Mulan were hard at work building something special. They had found an old crate and were attaching wheels to the bottom.

"Do you think this plan of yours will work?" Aurora asked Mulan.

Mulan nodded. "I hope so."

That's when they heard the rest of the princesses scream. They looked at each other, both knowing that wasn't a good sign.

Then they ran out of the kitchen, leaving their project half finished.

The princesses rushed out of the ballroom into the hallway, closing the door behind them. They could still hear the dragon inside, flying around, crashing into things.

Just then, Rapunzel noticed a piece of paper sticking out from under the fancy rug.

BOOM!
OOM!
CRASH!
Beware!
The dragon
is not a pet!

She picked it up. "It's from the Mysterious Messenger!" Rapunzel announced.

They gathered around to look.

"'Beware,'" Rapunzel read aloud. "'The dragon is not a pet.'"

"That would have been nice to know *earlier*!" Ariel cried.

The kitchen doors at the other end of the hallway flew open, and Mulan and Aurora ran out.

"Are you okay?" Mulan asked. "We heard screaming."

Cinderella sighed. "Yes. But the dragon is ruining the new ballroom!"

"I think she's just scared," Belle said.

"We have to find a way to get her out of the castle," said Jasmine, showing Mulan and Aurora the note from the Mysterious Messenger.

Mulan and Aurora looked at each other. "Actually, we're already working on that," Aurora said. "Come help us!"

The princesses followed Mulan and Aurora back into the kitchen.

With the help of all the princesses, the project was quickly completed.

"I call it the Cupcake Cart," said Aurora.

The princesses had built a beautiful wheeled cart. On it, they had placed twenty perfectly frosted cupcakes.

"Who's going to wheel it into the ballroom?" asked Ariel, looking scared.

Cinderella raised her hand. "I'll do it. This slumber party was my idea, after all. I should be the one to fix it."

"Let's just hope this works!" exclaimed Ariel.

Cinderella took a deep breath and pushed the Cupcake Cart down the long hallway toward the ballroom. She could still hear the dragon crashing into things behind the door.

Cinderella slowly opened the door. Then she pushed the cart through the ballroom, avoiding the flailing dragon, and opened the large doors to the garden. She then shoved the cart outside.

The dragon stopped and sniffed the air.

She could smell the delicious cupcakes, and she followed the Cupcake Cart right into the garden.

Cinderella quickly shut the garden door behind the dragon. The princesses all ran into the ballroom.

"Phew!" said Snow White.

"That was close!" said Rapunzel.

"I'm glad it worked," said Cinderella.

But Ariel was looking out the window at the dragon with a frown. "But won't she be sad?"

"I hope we didn't hurt her feelings by kicking her out," said Belle.

"But she's a *dragon*," said Aurora. "She doesn't belong inside a castle."

Ariel suddenly had another thought. She turned to the other princesses. "Maybe she just doesn't belong in *our* castle!" she said to the others.

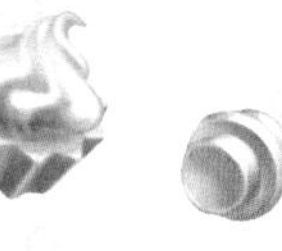

CHAPTER 14

While Belle, Rapunzel, Aurora, and Jasmine stayed behind to keep an eye on the dragon, Mulan, Snow White, Ariel, and Cinderella set off into the woods.

Then, while the dragon was still eating the last of the delicious cupcakes, the four princesses snuck into her lair and quickly got to work.

Snow White built a small wall outside for the dragon to sit on.

Ariel built a fountain for the dragon to splash in.

Cinderella built a dessert tray for the dragon to eat from.

And Mulan built a majestic pagoda for the dragon to lounge in.

When they were done, the dragon's lair had been completely transformed.

Even though the dragon had just eaten twenty delicious cupcakes, she still felt bad about what had happened. She knew the princesses were disappointed that she had burnt their marshmallows and knocked down all their decorations.

But she couldn't help it. She was a dragon!

As she slowly walked back to her lair, head hung low, she wondered if the princesses would ever invite her back to the castle again.

She doubted it.

And that made her feel worse.

By the time the dragon reached the part of the forest where she lived, she had already begun to cry.

"Shh!" said Cinderella. "She's coming!"

The four princesses were hiding behind a rock near the dragon's cave.

The dragon looked sad, but as soon as she saw the doorway of her cave, which was now decorated with twinkly fairy lights and strands of colorful flowers, she stopped.

Her giant dragon tail began to swish excitedly.

The princesses giggled.

The dragon ran into her new castle, and a moment later, the princesses heard a squeal of delight. Well, a dragon's version of a squeal.

"She loves it!" Mulan said.

"It worked!" Cinderella cried.

"I think we can all agree now that the dragon is not a pet," Snow White added.

"YES!" they all shouted at once.

But when they got back to the castle, Ariel was still frowning.

"What's wrong?" asked Belle.

"I still feel bad that we kicked her out of our party," replied Ariel.

"I have an idea!" Mulan said for the third time that day.

"Let's throw a surprise party in the forest for the dragon!"

"YES!" her friends shouted.

Then, suddenly, there was a loud knock on the door.

THUMP! THUMP! THUMP!

Jasmine opened the door to find the Mysterious Messenger standing there.

“NEVER SURPRISE A DRAGON!” the Mysterious Messenger said, winking. Then she turned to leave.

The princesses all looked at each other.

“Okay, maybe not,” said Mulan, and everyone laughed.

First Paperback Edition, October 2018
1 3 5 7 9 10 8 6 4 2
ISBN 978-1-368-02415-0
FAC-029261-18257

Library of Congress Control Number: 2018936689

Designed by Margie Peng

Printed in the United States of America